Family

La famille

lah fah-*mee*

Illustrated by Clare Beaton

Illustré par Clare Beaton

BARRON'S

mother

mom

la mère

lah mehr

maman

mah-*mah*

father
daddy

le père

leh pehr

papa

pah-*pah*

parents

les parents

leh pah-*rahn*

sister

la sœur

lah suhr

brother

le frère

leh frehr

uncle

l'oncle

lohnkl

aunt

la tante

lah tahnt

cousins

les cousins

leh coo-*zah*

grandmother
grandma

la grand-mère

lah groh-*mehr*

mémé

meh-*meh*

grandfather
grandpa

le grand-père

leh groh-*pehr*

pépé

peh-*peh*

grandparents

les grands-parents

leh groh-pah-*rahn*

A simple guide to pronouncing French words

- Read this guide as naturally as possible, as if it were English.
- Put stress on the letters in *italics*, for example, *mehr* in groh-*mehr*.
- Remember that the final consonants in French generally are silent (maman: mah-*mah*).

La famille	lah fah-*mee*	**Family**
la mère	lah mehr	**mother**
maman	mah-*mah*	**mom**
le père	leh pehr	**father**
papa	pah-*pah*	**daddy**
les parents	leh pah-*rahn*	**parents**
la sœur	lah suhr	**sister**
le frère	leh frehr	**brother**
l'oncle	lohnkl	**uncle**
la tante	lah tahnt	**aunt**
les cousins	leh coo-*zah*	**cousins**
la grand-mère	lah groh-*mehr*	**grandmother**
mémé	meh-*meh*	**grandma**
le grand-père	leh groh-*pehr*	**grandfather**
pépé	peh-*peh*	**grandpa**
les grands-parents	leh groh-pah-*rahn*	**grandparents**

Address all inquiries to: Barron's Educational Series, Inc., 250 Wireless Boulevard, Hauppauge, New York 11788.

International Standard Book Number 0-7641-0041-6

Library of Congress Catalog Card Number 96-85789

Printed in Hong Kong   987654321